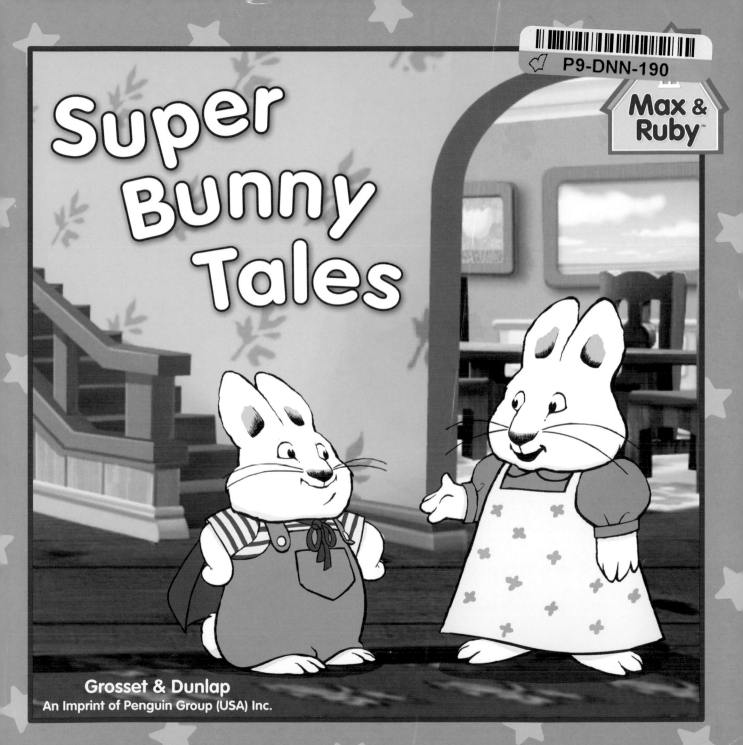

Super Bunny Tales

Max & Ruby™

Grosset & Dunlap
An Imprint of Penguin Group (USA) Inc.

GROSSET & DUNLAP
Published by the Penguin Group
Penguin Group (USA) Inc., 375 Hudson Street, New York, New York 10014, USA
Penguin Group (Canada), 90 Eglinton Avenue East, Suite 700,
Toronto, Ontario M4P 2Y3, Canada
(a division of Pearson Penguin Canada Inc.)
Penguin Books Ltd., 80 Strand, London WC2R 0RL, England
Penguin Group Ireland, 25 St. Stephen's Green, Dublin 2, Ireland
(a division of Penguin Books Ltd.)
Penguin Group (Australia), 250 Camberwell Road, Camberwell, Victoria 3124, Australia
(a division of Pearson Australia Group Pty. Ltd.)
Penguin Books India Pvt. Ltd., 11 Community Centre, Panchsheel Park,
New Delhi—110 017, India
Penguin Group (NZ), 67 Apollo Drive, Rosedale, North Shore 0632, New Zealand
(a division of Pearson New Zealand Ltd.)
Penguin Books (South Africa) (Pty.) Ltd., 24 Sturdee Avenue,
Rosebank, Johannesburg 2196, South Africa

Penguin Books Ltd., Registered Offices:
80 Strand, London WC2R 0RL, England

Based upon the animated series Max & Ruby
A Nelvana Limited production © 2002–2003.

Library of Congress Cataloging-in-Publication Data is available.

ISBN 978-0-448-45271-5   10 9 8 7 6 5 4 3 2 1

"It's a great day for a picnic, Max!" said Max's sister,
Ruby. "Time to get ready. Max, where are you?"

Max was listening to his favorite radio program, *Super Bunny*. He even had on his special red cape.

Max zoomed into the room. He nearly knocked Ruby down.
"Super Bunny!" shouted Max.
"No more Super Bunny! It's almost picnic time," said Ruby.

"Max, Sally Swimmer is coming to our picnic, too," said Ruby. "But I still need a few more things before I am ready."

"Super Bunny!" shouted Max.
As Max ran out of the room, he bumped into Ruby again!
Her picnic blanket flew up in the air.

The blanket fell on Sally. It popped her right into the picnic basket.
But Ruby didn't see it happen.

"Okay, Max. It's time to go," said Ruby. "You can pretend to be Super Bunny after the picnic."

"Oh no! Where's Sally Swimmer?" asked Ruby. "I left her on the table and now she is gone!"
Max didn't know where Sally Swimmer was.

11

Ruby looked for Sally in the kitchen and in the living room.
She could not find her.

Ruby looked in her bedroom, too. Sally was not with her other dollies.

"Where could she be?" asked Ruby.

13

"Max," said Ruby, "a real superhero would help me find Sally."

"Super Bunny!" shouted Max.

And off he went to search.

"Super Bunny!" shouted Max.
As Max zoomed through the dining room, he bumped into the picnic basket.
Out popped Sally Swimmer!

Max caught Sally Swimmer in midair!

"Thanks, Max. You really are a super bunny!" said Ruby.

"Let's play circus," said Louise.
"Yes!" said Ruby. "My Emily doll can be the star of the show."

19

Max zoomed into the room. He was pretending to be Super Bunny!
Ruby and Louise were too busy to play with Max.

Just then, Max saw that his toy train was going to crash into a stack of blocks!

"Save you!" said Max.
    Max and his sidekick, Red Rubber Elephant, blasted through the blocks.

Meanwhile, Ruby and Louise were upstairs.
"We need a big, white horse for Emily to ride in on," said Louise.
"But we don't have one," Ruby said.

"Max!" said Ruby. "Come be the audience for our circus!"
But Max didn't want to watch the circus. He zoomed right
out of the room.

But he left his elephant behind.
"Look, Louise!" said Ruby. "Emily can ride in on Max's elephant."

When Max zoomed back into the living room, his elephant was gone.

He looked all over the house.
Where was Red Rubber Elephant?
Then Max spotted it in the backyard.

"Save you!" said Max.

But Ruby took the elephant back.
"It's circus time, not Super Bunny time," said Ruby. "We need your elephant, Max."

"Attention! Emily the Amazing and her Rare Red
Elephant are on the trapeze!" shouted Ruby.
But Max didn't want his elephant on the trapeze.
"Save you!" said Max.

When Max grabbed his elephant back, he accidentally knocked Emily off the trapeze.
"Oh no!" said Ruby. "We forgot a safety net!"

"Save you!" said Max.
Max tossed his elephant right under Emily. She landed
safely on its back!

"Way to go!" said Louise.
"You saved the circus, Max!" cheered Ruby.

Max was listening to his favorite radio program, *Super Bunny.*
Max liked to pretend that he was a superhero, too.

In the kitchen, Ruby and Louise were working on their science fair project.

"We can make the solar system out of balloons," said Ruby.

"Rescue!" said Max.
"We don't need rescuing," said Ruby. "We are working."

So Max went into the living room. He wound up all his toys.

Max's lobster chased his chicks right out of the room.
"Rescue!" said Max.
He followed the lobster and the chicks into the kitchen.

Whoops! Max bumped into Ruby and Louise.
The girls got papier-mâché all over their noses.
"Be careful, Max!" said Ruby. "We don't want our project to break."

Max ran after the lobster and the chicks.
"Rescue!" said Max.
He scooped up all the chicks. Now the lobster couldn't reach them.

In the kitchen, Ruby and Louise were done covering the balloons.

"Now we'll paint them to look like planets!" said Louise.

Meanwhile, Max was wondering where his lobster went.

Ruby and Louise finished making the solar system.
"Isn't our world beautiful?" asked Ruby.
"It sure is," said Louise.

Suddenly Max's lobster crawled into the kitchen.
"Max, come get your lobster!" said Ruby. "We don't
want it to ruin our project."

45

But the lobster nipped at Ruby's feet.
Ruby jumped. The Earth went flying out of her hands.

"Rescue!" shouted Max.
He caught the Earth just before it crashed to the floor.

47

"Look, Max! You rescued the world!" said Ruby.